For my family
~SC

To Michael MacSwiney affectionately
~NB

First American edition published 2000 by

Crocodile Books, USA

An imprint of Interlink Publishing Group, Inc.

99 Seventh Avenue • Brooklyn, New York 11215 and
46 Crosby Street • Northampton, Massachusetts 01060

Published simultaneously in Great Britain by Little Tiger Press,
an imprint of Magi Publications, London

Text © 2000 Sheridan Cain • Illustrations © 2000 Norma Burgin

Library of Congress Cataloging-in-Publication Data

Cain, Sheridan.

Little Turtle and the song of the sea / Sheridan Cain ;
illustrated by Norma Burgin.
p. cm.

Summary: Little Turtle hatches on the beach and struggles to make a
perilous journey down to the sea.

ISBN 1-56656-355-0

1. Sea turtles—Juvenile fiction [1. Sea turtles—Fiction. 2. Turtles—Fiction.]
I. Burgin, Norma. ill. II. Title. PZ10.3.C135 Ci 2000
[E]—dc21 99-053456

LITTLE TURTLE
and the Song of the Sea

SHERIDAN CAIN

Illustrated by NORMA BURGIN

DISCARD

Crocodile Books, USA
An imprint of Interlink Publishing Group, Inc.
NEW YORK

Beneath the sand Little Turtle lay curled tightly in his egg. He could hear the *SWISH, SWISH, SWISH* of the Sea up above him.

Little Turtle stretched and wiggled. Soon his eggshell began to crack, and the sand trickled down around him.

"Come, Little Turtle," sang the Sea. "Come, Little Turtle, come home to me."

But the sand became heavy, pressing down on Little Turtle until he thought he would be squashed.

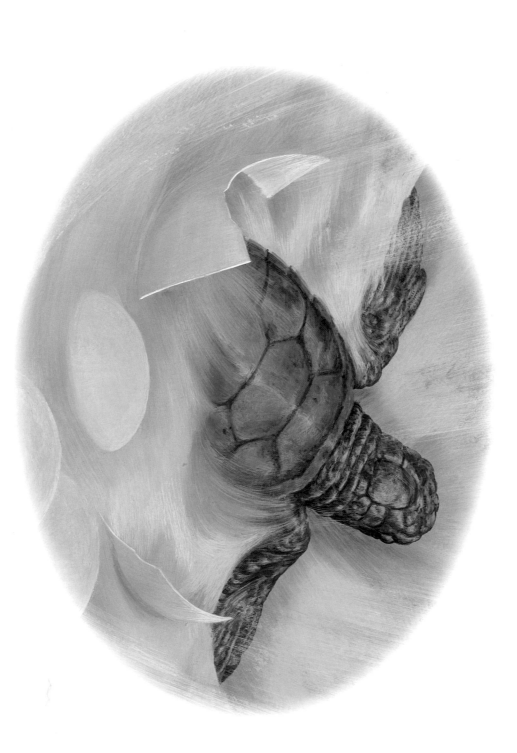

"Push, Little Turtle," sang the Sea. "Push, Little Turtle, and you'll soon be free."

Little Turtle pushed and scooped with his tiny flippers until they ached. Then, with a big heave, he pulled himself up.

All around him he saw the bright twinkling light of the stars.

"Well done, Little Turtle," sang the Sea. "Now, Little Turtle, hurry home to me."

Little Turtle did not know which way to go. He was afraid, for the world looked so big.

"Turn, Little Turtle," sang the Sea. *"Turn towards the brightness that shines on me."*

Little Turtle turned, and as he did so, he saw the round glow of the sun rising upon the Sea.

Little Turtle went towards the sun, but he heard a sharp cry, and the dark shape of a seagull swooped towards him.

"*Run, Little Turtle,*" sang the Sea. "*Run towards the rocks, and safe you'll be.*"

Little Turtle turned towards the rocks with the wind from Seagull's wings beating close behind him.

He scrambled between the rocks to safety, and Seagull flew off with an angry "YAAAAK."

Little Turtle heard a scratching, scraping sound. His eyes became wide, as a huge claw appeared from under the rock.

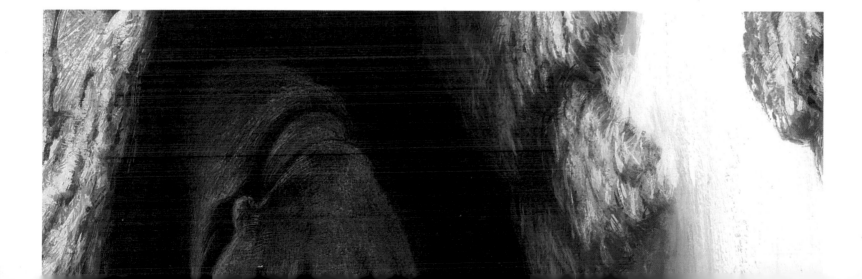

Crab scuttled out, snapping and threatening Little Turtle with his huge pincer.

"Look out, Little Turtle," sang the Sea. "Hurry, Little Turtle, hurry home to me."

Crab lunged towards him. There was a sharp nip at his tail, but Little Turtle was too fast—and the disappointed Crab crawled back under his rock.

"Come on, Little Turtle," sang the Sea.
"A few more steps, and safe you'll be."

But Little Turtle was tired, and he could
go no further. He lay in the sand, just
out of reach of the Sea.

"I'm coming, Little Turtle," called the Sea. She stretched her watery arms toward him. With one last effort, Little Turtle stretched out his flippers . . .

and the Sea lifted him gently onto her waves.

"*Welcome home, Little Turtle,*" sighed the Sea.

"At last," sang Little Turtle, "at last I'm free."